CREEPY CREATURES

igloo

Night of the Full Moon

It was a cold, dark, night and the Brown family were lost. Their car had juddered to a halt outside the gates of a large country house. Mr Brown shook his head in disbelief. "We'll just have to ask for help at that old house," said Mrs Brown. In the back of the car, their two sons, Ed and Matthew, rolled their eyes, as if they were really bored by the idea.

A few moments later, the Browns stood in the crumbling porch of Upshire Hall. "Can I ring the bell?" said Matthew, reaching out and tugging an old-fashioned bell-pull. A deep, mournful ringing sound echoed from beyond the door. The Brown family looked at one another.

"What a weird noise," said Ed, looking up at the grim walls of the foreboding house. "The mad butler is going to open the door any minute. We're all going to die!" "Be quiet," shushed Mrs Brown, "someone's coming."

Footsteps echoed from inside. The huge, oak door creaked open. An elderly man stood in the doorway, holding a dusty old candelabra. "Good evening," he said, "I didn't expect any visitors, especially not tonight. I'm Lord Upshire. Do come in, it's not safe out there."

"What does he mean, 'not safe'?" whispered Mrs Brown, as the family shuffled inside. Suits of armour lined the walls and the hall had the smell and feel of somewhere that had been long neglected.

"Sorry to trouble you, My Lord," said Mr Brown. "I wondered if I might use your phone? Our car just stopped suddenly, right outside the gates of your house.

Lord Upshire nodded, knowingly. "It's the full moon," he said. "Strange things always happen here when there's a full moon. Nothing will work until tomorrow, I'm afraid, no phones and no electricity. The place is cursed, you know. Even the staff have left. It's just me here, now." He lifted the candelabra and the candles flickered dimly around the bleak hall.

Lord Upshire shrugged his shoulders and smiled. "You'll all have to stay here tonight. I can't let you go wandering off outside, the cats will be out soon." The Brown family glanced at each other. Why should cats be a problem?

Night of the Full Moon

After giving them something to eat, Lord Upshire showed the family to their bedrooms. "You must bolt your door," he warned the boys. "Do not open it under any circumstances." Then he handed them a candle and shuffled off to bed.

Ed and Matthew's room was creepy and smelled of mushrooms, like an ancient museum. The sheets were cold and the boys were too scared to close their eyes. Suddenly, there was a noise outside, in the hallway. The boys sat bolt upright in bed. The noise was a throaty, gurgling growl.

Despite Lord Upshire's warning, Ed opened the door and the boys peered down the gloomy corridor. There was nothing there. The noise came again, this time it was further away. "It's coming from the long gallery," said Matthew.

Night of the Full Moon

The brothers crept slowly forwards and the candle flickered eerily in the damp, drafty hallway. The gallery was silent. Around the room and on the walls, the stuffed bodies and heads of big cats glared silently. "It's like a dead jungle," whispered Matthew.

Suddenly, something moved on the floor by the fireplace. It seemed to wriggle and shift and then it began to grow. The boys stared in disbelief. A tiger-skin rug was moving. "It's coming to life," gasped Ed.

The striped body rose upwards to its full size. It shook itself and looked around. The boys froze, as the tiger looked straight at them. The big cat bared huge teeth and let out a terrible roar. The whole room seemed to shake.

The boys shrank backwards and inched slowly along the wall as the tiger, its eyes glinting, followed them. It crouched and got ready to spring. Ed and Matthew waited, frozen with fear.

Night of the Full Moon

Suddenly, all the big cats began to move. A black panther hissed and crouched. Lions and a cougar surrounded the boys. There was no way out. The cats came closer and closer. They were stalking their prey.

Ed and Matthew shrank back. They pressed themselves against the wooden panels that lined the walls. Suddenly, there was a slight 'click' and a panel gave way. The brothers fell backwards, landing with a thud, as the secret wooden door snapped in front of them. Outside, there was a fierce yowling and scratching.

"Where are we?" asked Ed. "Some sort of secret room," replied Matthew.

The boys looked around. Light filtered through tiny ridges in the wood. In the corner, they saw a wooden tube that was covered in dust. Ed reached over and opened it. Inside, was a paper scroll. He unravelled it and began to read. "It says that on each full moon, the animal spirits shall come alive. This is a curse cast upon the Upshire family for years of hunting big cats. The only way to break the curse is for the cats to be outside when the sun rises." The boys looked at each other. "We've got to tell Lord Upshire," they said together.

The boys carefully opened the secret door. The cats had escaped from the house and were prowling outside. The boys ran down the long corridors and banged on the bedroom doors, to wake everyone up.

Lord Upshire read the scroll. "It has been lost for years," he said. "Now we know how to lift the curse. Come on, everyone, lock all the doors and windows."

Outside, the big cats paced and yowled. The sun was beginning to rise and as it did, each cat gradually began to fade away.

By the time the sun was full in the sky, the cats were gone forever. "Your car will work now," said Lord Upshire to Mr and Mrs Brown. "As for these two brave boys, they will be remembered as the gallant knights who lifted the curse of Upshire Hall."

Matthew and Ed smiled at each other. They couldn't wait to get back home. No one at school was ever going to believe their amazing adventure on the night of the full moon.

Lair of the Wolfman

It was a sunny day at Monster World Theme Park. Jess, Jake, Ella and Max had just been on the fastest ride ever. "My legs are wobbling," said Ella. "I feel sick," moaned Jess.

Max smiled and looked at Jake. "I think we'd better go on something a bit quieter next," he said and pointed at a big tunnel in the shape of a huge skull. An empty carriage rattled towards the skull's open mouth and stopped near the entrance. "Let's go on the ghost train," said Jake.

The four friends scrambled into the open carriage. The boys jumped into the front, determined to get the best view. "I don't like being at the back," said Jess, "What if we get grabbed?"

The boys just laughed. "It's not real, Jess," said Max, "It's just a bit of fun." Suddenly, the carriage gave a jolt and moved forward into the darkness. Ella looked back to see the sunlit park disappearing behind them.

The tunnel was dark and cold. Nothing moved except the train, which inched forward slowly. "I can't see a thing," said Ella. Her heart pounded. In the pitch black, something hairy brushed past her face. She let out an ear-splitting scream and the boys covered their ears.

A flicker of light revealed cobwebs hanging from the ceiling and a hairy spider that bobbed up and down on a piece of elastic. Rubber bats swooped low and tattered, giant moths dangled from the roof of the tunnel. "It's so fake," said Max, "it's got to be the oldest ride in the park."

Lair of the Wolfman

The lights began to flicker dimly, as the train track curved into a cave mouth. Above the entrance was a sign that said, *Lair of the Wolfman*. "Oh, no!" cried Jake, in mock horror. "Please, not the Wolfman!"

The train moved into a large chamber that was made to look like a forest. A full moon glowed in the darkness. The sound of distant wolf howls echoed from hidden speakers, as the little train edged further into the cave.

Up ahead, the moonlight pooled around a shadowy figure, crouched near a clump of trees. The body was bent, as if on all fours, yet strangely twisted and hunched. Coarse hair covered the thick, muscular body. The creature's huge head hung low and its blood-shot eyes stared forward, blankly.

Lair of the Wolfman

The friends stared at the beast. The boys burst out laughing. "It's pathetic," said Jake. However, Jess wasn't laughing and neither was Ella. They didn't think the creature was funny at all. Those vacant, bloodied eyes gave them the creeps. "I want to get out of here," whispered Jess.
"Me, too," said Ella.

The train moved on. Darkness enveloped the carriage and, just as it left the cave, the girls turned to look at the beast. They gasped in horror - its head was turned in their direction and it was looking straight at them.

Lair of the Wolfman

In the tunnel, the train stopped and the lights went out. The boys clapped their hands. "Fantastic," they said together, expecting some scary fun.

The girls however, were silent. Suddenly, the tunnel began to echo with noises. There was an odd, padding sound, like muffled steps, then a gurgle and a moan. Suddenly, the boys were thrust forward, so much that they almost toppled out of the carriage. A terrible scream rang out, then there was silence. Something laughed and it didn't sound like an animal, or a human. It was savage and chilling.

The lights flickered on. "Wow!" said Jake, looking at Max, "That's more like it. What do you think, girls?" he said, turning round. But the seats behind them were empty. The girls had gone.

"Where are they?" said Max.
"They must have got out," replied Jake, in an anxious voice, "We'll have to get out and look for them."

The boys were beginning to feel uneasy. They got out of the train and walked carefully down the tunnel. The track led back to the lair of the Wolfman. It felt strange and creepy.

Inside the lair, the moon still glowed above the trees, it was unnaturally quiet. There was a scuffling sound from the dark. "What was that?" whispered Jake, clutching Max's arm.
Next, they heard a gasp, then a stifled scream.

In the moonlight, the boys saw the shape of the beast. His head tilted back and he let out a long, slow howl. It was the howl of a hunter with its prey. Jess and Ella were huddled nearby, terrified.

Suddenly, the light of the full moon began to dim. It seemed to make the Wolfman weak. He sank to his knees, howling in pain. Jake seized the opportunity and darted forward to free the girls.

"Quick," shouted Max, "run for it!"

The four friends ran through the dim lair. Behind them, the Wolfman growled and gnashed his teeth. Suddenly, the moon began to glow again and the Wolfman became strong. He howled and his red eyes flashed, furiously.

Lair of the Wolfman

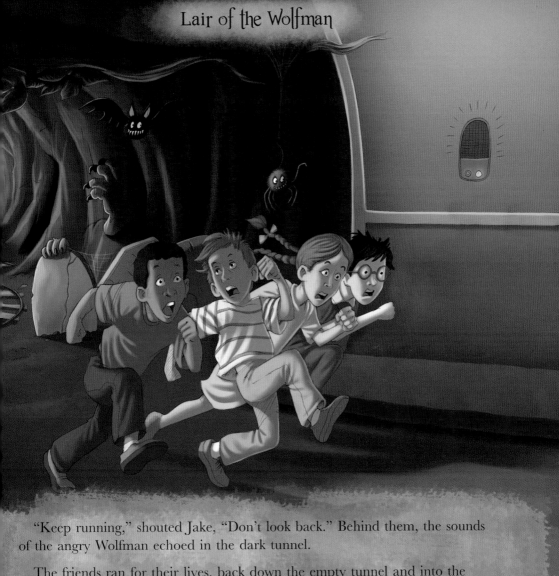

"Keep running," shouted Jake, "Don't look back." Behind them, the sounds of the angry Wolfman echoed in the dark tunnel.

The friends ran for their lives, back down the empty tunnel and into the sunlight. "Wow!" said Max, gasping for breath. "Was that real?"
"We're not going back in to find out." said the Jess.
"Let's go back on the fast ride," said Ella, "It'll be a breeze after the 'Lair of the Wolfman'!"

Tunnel of Terror

One cold evening, Mark and his friends, Joel and Dan, were travelling home from school on the underground train. The train was just beginning to slow, on its approach to the next station, when something caught Mark's eye. A shape was moving in the tunnel. "Did you see that?" asked Mark, "There's something out there, in the tunnel."

The boys didn't take any notice. "Yeah, right," said Joel, without even looking up from his game console. "Everyone knows that you're always seeing monsters where there aren't any."

But Mark knew he had seen something, slithering along, in the dark tunnel. It had a long, worm-like body, with lots of legs. Mark was determined to find out what it was. "I'm going after it!" he said.

"Suit yourself," laughed Joel, "We've got to change trains anyway because they're doing repairs at this station." Just as he spoke, the train slowed to a halt at the platform.

As the last passengers made their way to the exit, Mark hid in a shadowy recess. He listened while the workers set up their equipment for the station repairs. When they eventually went for their evening break, Mark grabbed one of their torches.

Suddenly, the platform was empty and eerily silent. Mark jumped onto the track and set off down the tunnel. It was dark and the small torch didn't light up much of the inky blackness. Mark thought he could hear something slithering towards him in the distance, but when he shone the torch, nothing was there.

Mark scanned the arched tunnel and found streaks of sticky, green slime glowing on the floor and walls. He followed the trail to a huge crack in the floor. As Mark peered into the crack, he could make out what looked like a tangle of shapes, writhing in the weak beam of light.

Suddenly, a noise came from the darkness behind him. Mark clicked off the torch, crept slowly forwards and was swallowed by the dense blackness. A foul stench filled his nostrils, Mark could sense that something was close by. He flicked on the torch and the pale light played over the shiny amber skin of something that appeared to be an enormous, sleeping, centipede.

Tunnel of Terror

Without thinking, Mark pulled out his camera from his pocket and took a picture. The camera flash was an explosion of light in the darkness. The startled creature reared up, its limbs waving chaotically, high above Mark's head. Huge, bulbous eyes glowed, like pale orbs. The thing let out a horrible, high-pitched screech. "Oh, no," said Mark in a panic, "That was a big mistake."

The creature began to uncoil its body. Mark turned and fled along the dark tunnel, back towards the station. Behind him, the monster began to move, it's multiple legs scuttling along the old train track.

Tunnel of Terror

Mark ran blindly onwards through the tunnel, which seemed endless. He ran until he felt his legs go weak. Suddenly he stumbled and fell. The walls echoed the terrifying clatter and rattle of scaly legs that were coming closer and closer.

Mark's blood ran cold, as he turned to see the wriggling underbelly of the gigantic beast rearing up in front of him. "I'm dead," he thought. The torch wasn't bright enough to deter it. Then he remembered the camera.

Quickly, Mark took a picture. The flash momentarily blinded the creature and it shrank back, squealing, allowing him to scramble away.

With shaking hands, the terrified boy shone the torch in front of him. The empty station was just visible up ahead. Heaving himself onto the platform, Mark stumbled and almost fell as he staggered up the motionless escalator.

"I should be safe, now," he thought, his mind racing. "I'll go and find the workmen." But then a scuttling sound echoed off the walls. The giant bug was right behind him. "I can't let it get to the surface," thought Mark. He was almost at the top of the escalator when he had an idea.

The central panel between the escalators made a perfect slide and Mark jumped onto it. There was no time to lose. He could not let the creature get into the outside world. "I must lead the bug back down to that crack in the ground," said Mark, as he slid past the angry creature, waving his torch. The huge bug snaked its long body back round and chased its prey down into the tunnels.

Mark stumbled in the dark and managed to find the crack in the ground. The lumbering creature was right behind him, as Mark jumped across the huge crack and dropped the torch into the blackness.